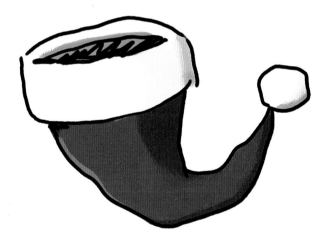

—

SANTA DUCK
AND HIS
MERRY HELPERS

DAVID MILGRIM

G. P. Putnam's Sons
An Imprint of Penguin Group (USA) Inc.

For Nancy Paulsen and Cecilia Yung,
with thanks for all the help and guidance!

G. P. PUTNAM'S SONS
A division of Penguin Young Readers Group.
Published by The Penguin Group.
Penguin Group (USA) Inc., 375 Hudson Street, New York, NY 10014, U.S.A.
Penguin Group (Canada), 90 Eglinton Avenue East, Suite 700, Toronto, Ontario M4P 2Y3, Canada
(a division of Pearson Penguin Canada Inc.).
Penguin Books Ltd, 80 Strand, London WC2R 0RL, England.
Penguin Ireland, 25 St. Stephen's Green, Dublin 2, Ireland (a division of Penguin Books Ltd.).
Penguin Group (Australia), 250 Camberwell Road, Camberwell, Victoria 3124, Australia
(a division of Pearson Australia Group Pty Ltd).
Penguin Books India Pvt Ltd, 11 Community Centre, Panchsheel Park, New Delhi - 110 017, India.
Penguin Group (NZ), 67 Apollo Drive, Rosedale, North Shore 0632, New Zealand
(a division of Pearson New Zealand Ltd).
Penguin Books (South Africa) (Pty) Ltd, 24 Sturdee Avenue, Rosebank,
Johannesburg 2196, South Africa.
Penguin Books Ltd, Registered Offices: 80 Strand, London WC2R 0RL, England.

Published simultaneously in Canada. Manufactured in China by South China Printing Co. Ltd.
Design by Marikka Tamura and Katrina Damkoehler. Text set in ATAdminister Bold.
The art was done in digital ink and digital oil pastel.

Library of Congress Cataloging-in-Publication Data
Milgrim, David.
Santa Duck and his merry helpers / David Milgrim.   p. cm.
Summary: Every Christmas, Nicholas Duck helps Santa by collecting gift lists,
but this year his little brothers and sister create havoc when they try to help,
leading Nicholas to contemplate the true meaning of Christmas.
[1. Christmas—Fiction. 2. Ducks—Fiction. 3. Brothers and sisters—Fiction.] I. Title.
PZ7.M5955San 2010   [E]—dc22   2009047517
ISBN 978-0-399-25473-4
1 3 5 7 9 10 8 6 4 2

Visit the author at his website:
www.davidmilgrim.com

Christmas was coming!
That meant it was time for
Nicholas Duck to put on
his official coat and hat
and help collect
wish lists for Santa.

He couldn't have been happier.

Then Nicholas realized
he was being followed.

It was his little brothers and sister.

Nicholas explained that you can't just *decide* to be Santa's helpers. He explained that it is a *very VERY special* position, and you have to be selected by Santa himself!

And since there was nothing
Nicholas could do to stop them,
he continued on his way.

Soon, Nicholas met a skunk.

Things got even worse with the raccoon.

And the beaver.

By the time they met the frog,
Nicholas could hardly take it anymore.

Nicholas tried to explain.

Then Nicholas explained
the true meaning of Christmas.

What could Nicholas say? His family was right.
Christmas was about letting them help Santa too.
Which is just what he did.

Santa thanked them all,
and the ducks went home.

And they ate popcorn balls and candy canes and sang Christmas songs all night long!